We're just passing the Dead Planet, Captain. I thought I saw something move.

You're just jumpy, Chuck; nobody could exist in that atmosphere...

Buzz checked their position — something was wrong. They were heading into a belt of asteroids...

Hey, you guys, the controls won't respond!

THIS PLANET WAS ABANDONED ON 10th JULY 1998

Falling Star Employment Agency

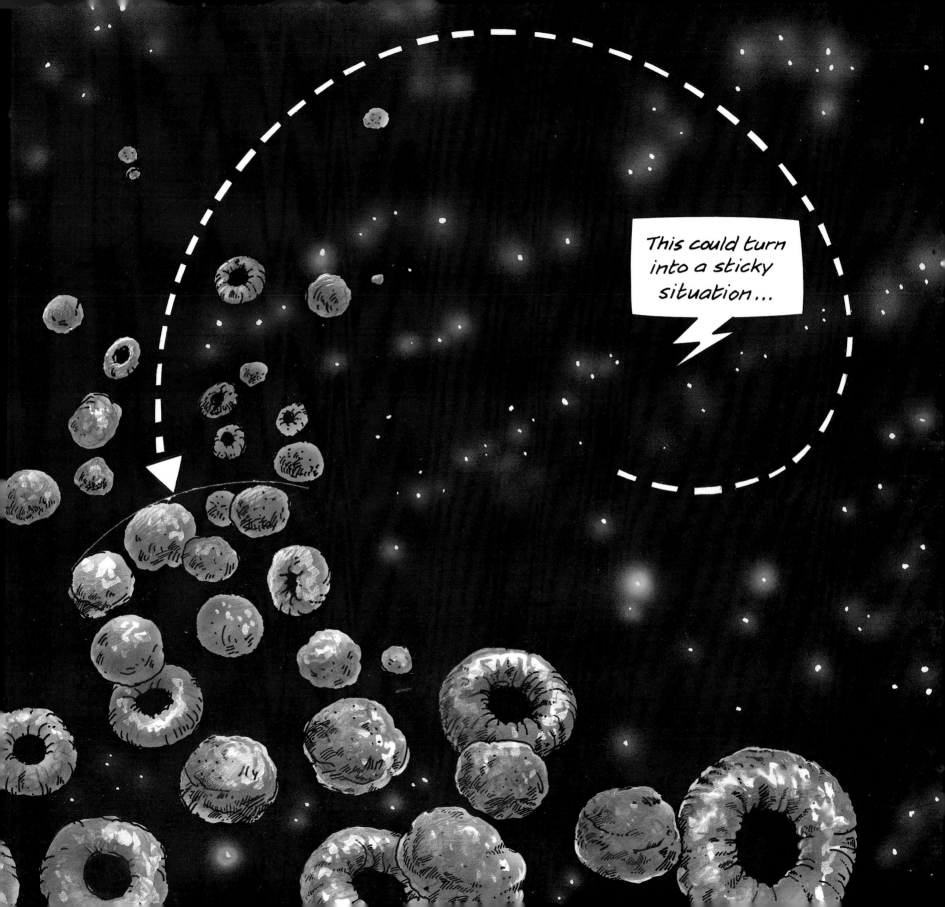

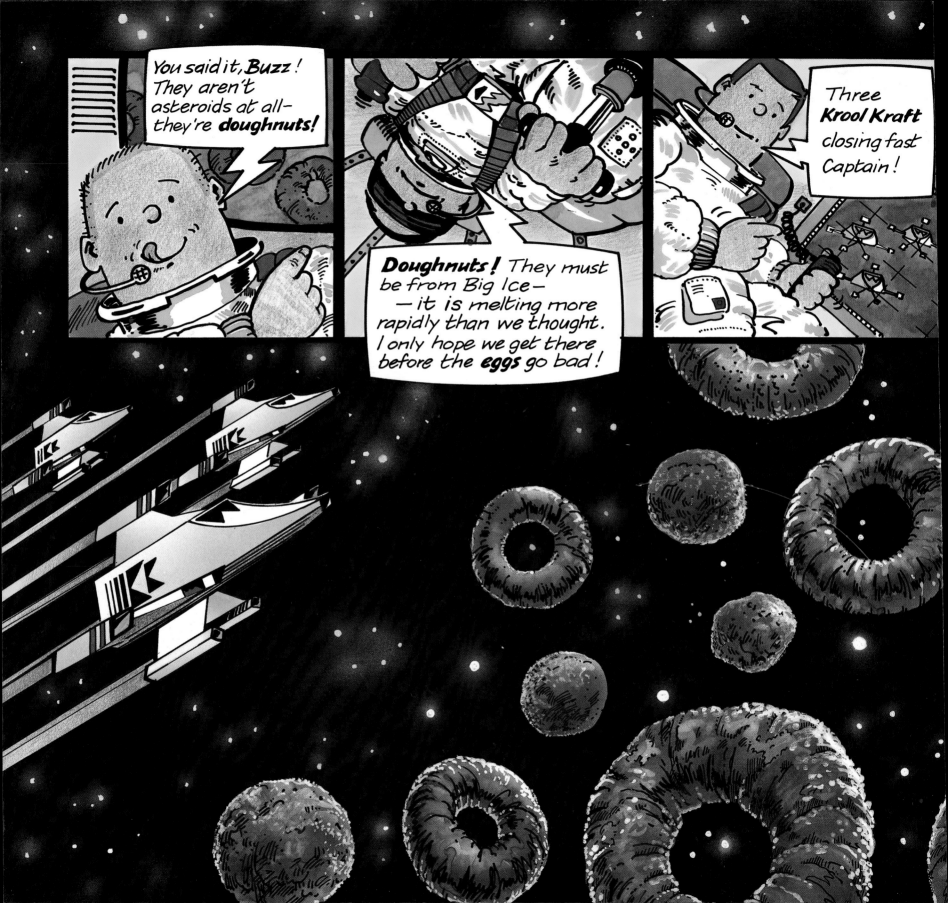

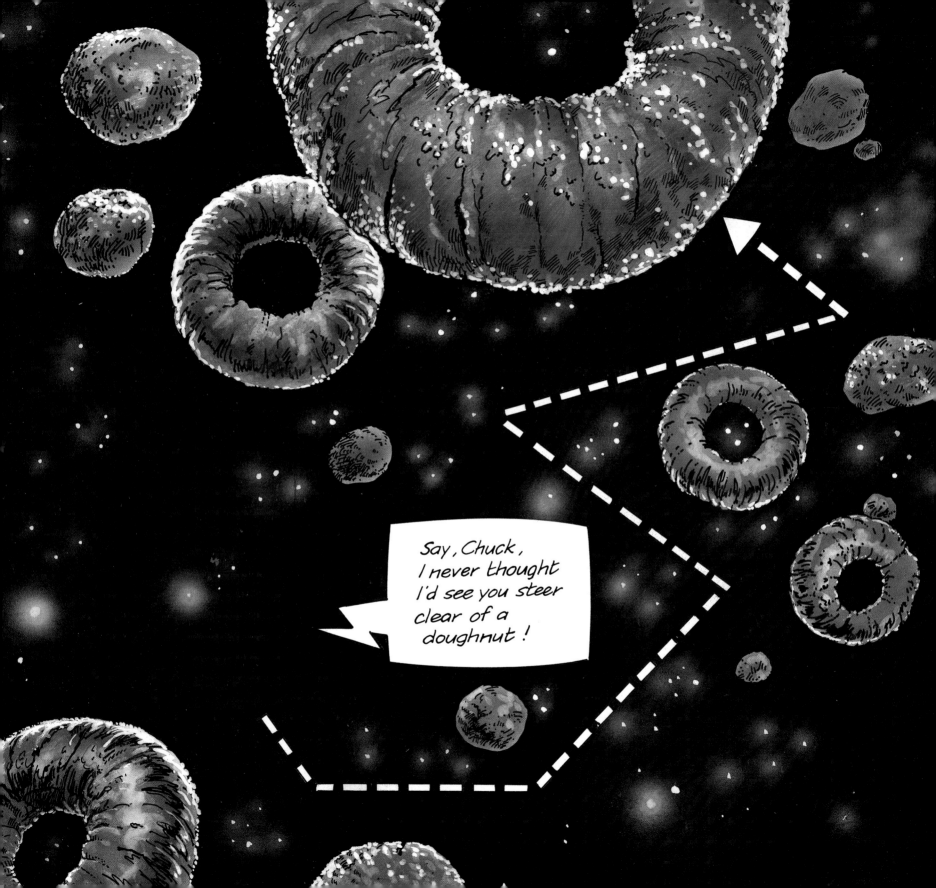

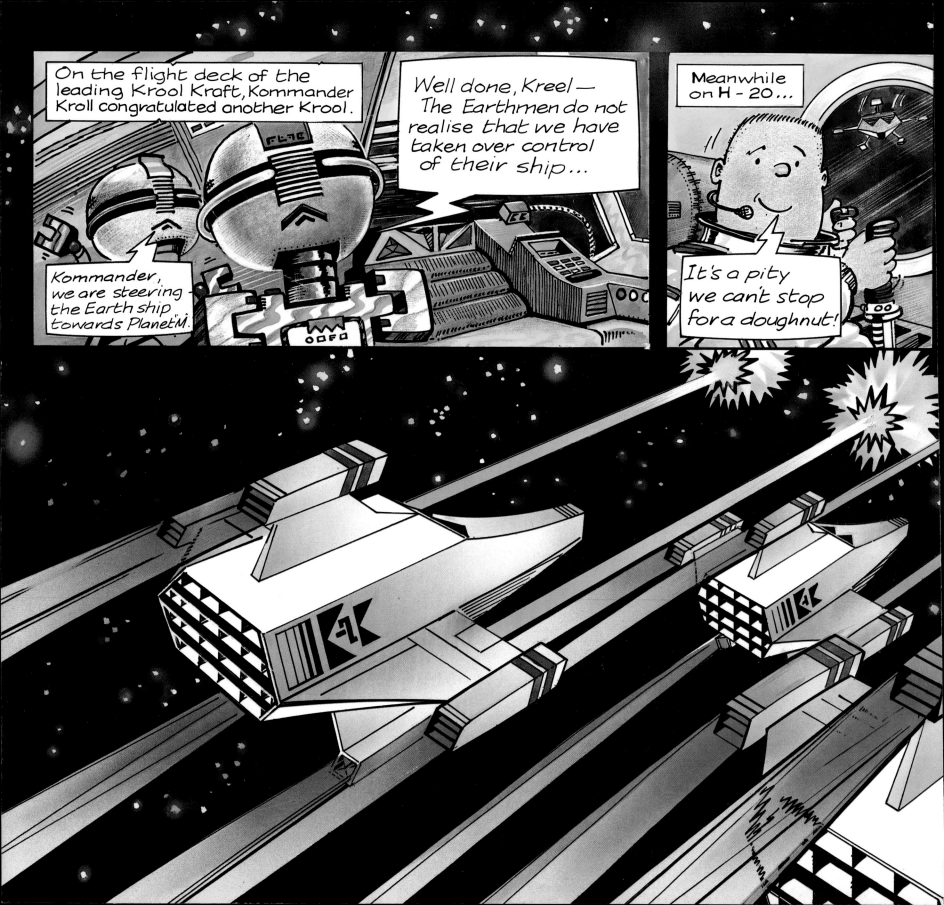

The Magnetic Planet (or Planet 'M') is a man-made device designed to attract all the unwanted and obsolete material drifting around in space. The Krools have cunningly increased the intensity of the magnetic force to such a degree that space craft like H-20 cannot resist its pull. This is how they have prevented previous missions from reaching Big Ice...

This looks bad... Obviously all the H-craft sent have ended up here on Planet 'M'.

If we don't get to Big Ice in the next few hours, there's going to be a universal mess?

Buzz was busy reading a book...

How can you sit reading at a time like this when all that food is going to waste?

Calm down, Chuck; this could be the answer to our problem. Early H-type craft are fitted with a dual polarity system...

Dual Polarity Facility.

Here it is, Buzz, under the floor covering...

Chuck pressed the button which reversed the magnetic pull of Planet 'M'.

Hey, you guys! It worked — we're moving again!

Big Ice here we come!

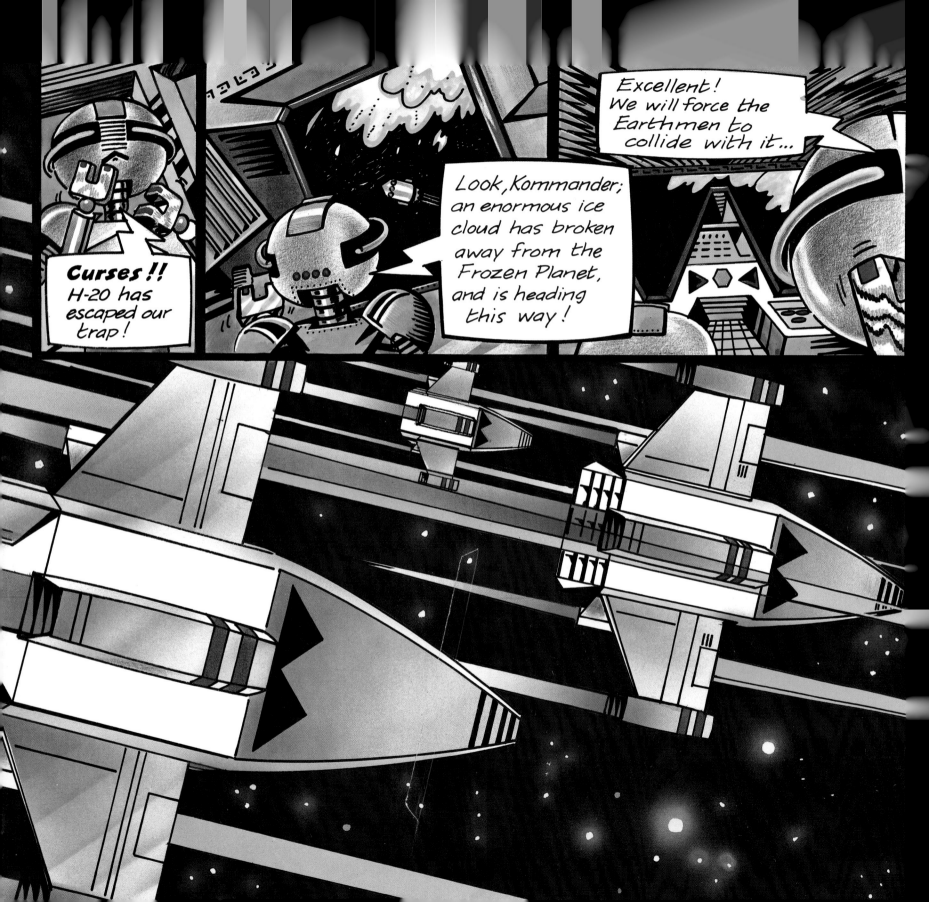